AUTHOR'S NOTE

At Christmastime, in the New Hampshire town where I live, it is traditional for white electric candles to be put in house windows and in the windows of the Baptist Church. It is a beautiful sight. But the early residents of this New England town and other villages weren't always so festive. Although Catholics, Episcopalians, Lutherans and some other settlers celebrated Christmas in church and out, the early Baptists, Presbyterians, Quakers, and Puritans tended to avoid any observance of the holiday whatsoever. In fact, one source tells of an Irishman being chased out of a New England town in 1755 because he was "a Christmas Man." All of this set me to thinking, "What *might* have happened in the early 1800s if a family accustomed to celebrating Christmas moved into a New England town?"

Using historical fact and my research as a departure point, I began to imagine that it could have happened this way . . .

T.DeP.
NEW HAMPSHIRE

AN
Early American
Christmas

written and illustrated by

Tomie dePaola

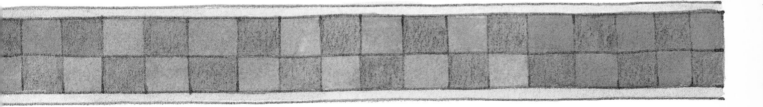

Holiday House : New York

*To all the Christmas families
in New London, New Hampshire*

Copyright © 1987 by Tomie dePaola
All rights reserved
Printed in the United States of America
First Edition

Library of Congress Cataloging-in-Publication Data

DePaola, Tomie.
An early American Christmas.

Summary: The inhabitants of a New England village
never make much fuss about Christmas until a new family
moves in and celebrates the holiday in a special way.
[1. Christmas—Fiction]   I. Title.
PZ7.D439Ear   1987   [E]   86-3102
ISBN 0-8234-0617-2

Once, a long time ago
in the small New England village,
not one single candle could be seen in the windows
at Christmastime.

Not an evergreen wreath on the door.

Not a Christmas tree in the parlor.

Not even a Christmas song could be heard
in the night air . . .

Until the family moved into the white farmhouse
down the road.
They had come first from faraway Germany
to faraway Pennsylvania and finally to this village.

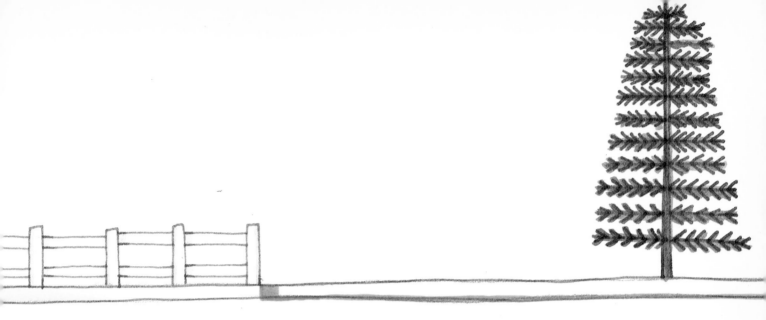

They celebrated Christmas,
so people called them "the Christmas Family."

In the fall of the year,
the young woman and the girl picked
the gray waxy berries
from the bayberry bushes in the field.
They picked and picked.

Then, they put the berries and some water
in the big black cauldron
that was set over a fire
in the kitchen dooryard.

While the old woman stirred and stirred,
the gray green wax formed,
and the young woman poured it into another kettle.

The two women tied strings on sticks
and dipped them into the wax.
They dipped and dipped and dipped some more
and soon the strings became candles—
candles made from bayberries that smelled oh-so-sweet
and that would burn at the windows
and on the mantelpiece at Christmastime.

"Bayberry candles bring good fortune
to any home where they shed their light,"
said the young woman.

"A bayberry candle burned to the socket
brings luck to the house, food to the larder,
and gold to the pocket," said the old woman.

In the fall of the year,
the young man and the boys gathered the apples
and the pumpkins and the squash,
and they dug the potatoes and put them away for the winter
in the root cellar.
The best apples, the reddest and the shiniest,
were set aside to be used at Christmastime.

The old man carved and whittled
while the baby watched—
a new figure for the manger scene.

As the days grew shorter, the winds blew colder.
Then the snow began to fly and December was here.
Soon, soon, it would be Christmas.

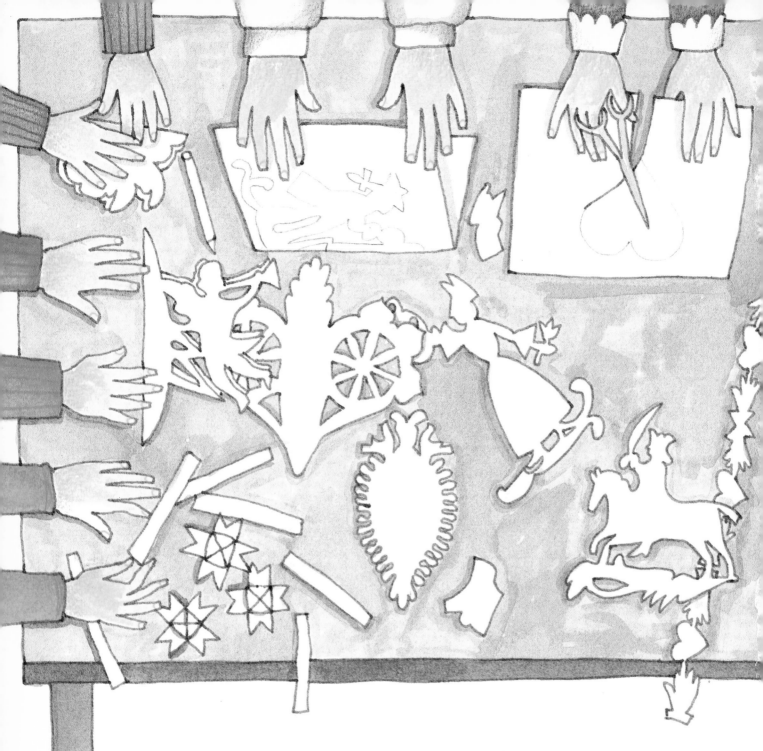

Around the fire the family sat
while scissors snipped out birds and ladies and gentlemen,
and riders on white horses, angels, pomegranates,
"hearts of man" and long bands—
all to trim the Christmas tree.
The girl folded paper into stars
to put on the bushes outside.
She waxed them to protect them from the snow.

The old man turned nuts into golden fruit
with a flick of his brush,
and the old woman baked the cookies
that would hang beside the golden nuts
on the tree.

Out in the meadow, by the edge of the woods,
the young man and the boys looked for a tree
to cut and bring inside when the time came.
They tied a red cloth to the top
so they would find it again.

Up from the root cellar came apples
to cut and to string and to dry
for garlands to put on the tree.
Corn was popped and set aside for a day,
and then it too was strung.

Then the baking for eating began
because Christmas was getting closer—
white cookies, brown cookies,
cookie ladies and cookie men,
cookies made with anise seed, honey cakes,
small pretzels and large pretzels—
pretzels everywhere.
Now, tulips, lovebirds, "hands-and-hearts,"
peacocks, and stars
filled the shelves and tables of the kitchen.

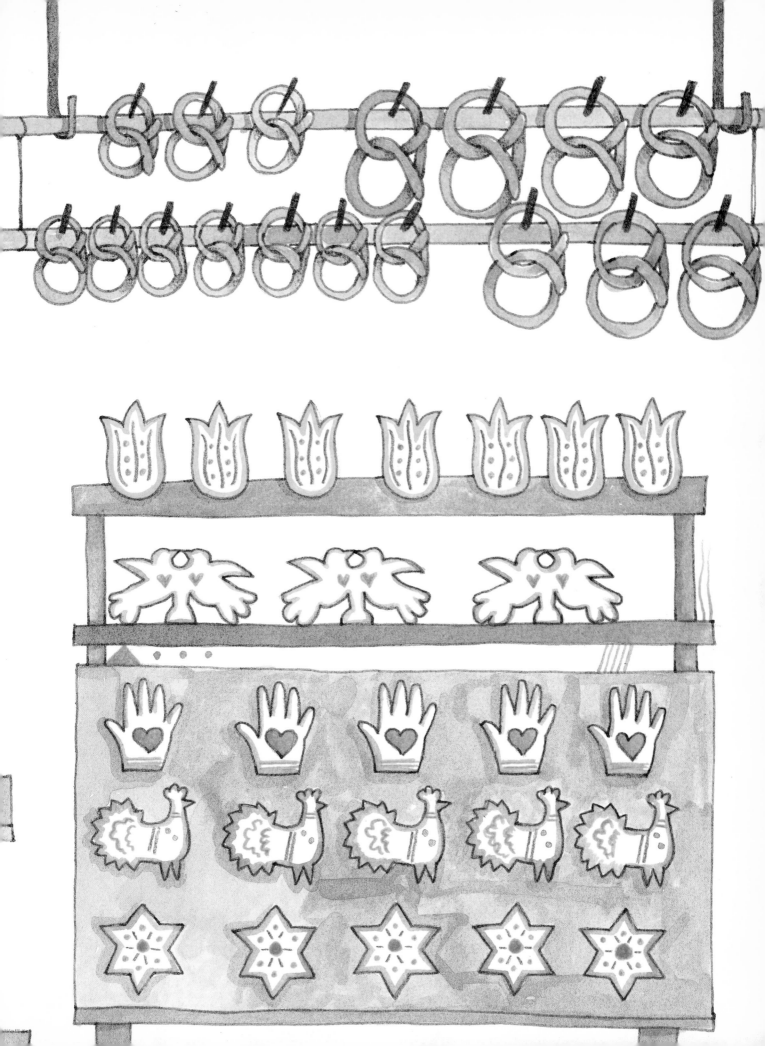

"It's time, it's time,"
   the young man called on the day before Christmas,
   and he and the boys went out to cut the tree
   and gather greens for the mantelpiece
   and the door and the windowsills.

The old man put together the wooden pieces
for the Christmas pyramid.

The old woman got out the figures
for the manger scene.

The young woman went to the root cellar
for the best apples,
and the girl gathered the candles
they had made so many days ago.

The baby banged her cup up and down,
for Christmas was almost here.

In came the tree, into the parlor.

"Quickly, quickly," the old woman said,
"put the greens around, decorate the tree,
set the manger scene up.
Candles on the mantelpiece, candles in each window,
greens on the door,
waxed paper stars on the bushes outside,
apples in a rosy pile,
cookies on platters and plates."

"It's time, it's time," the young woman called.
"It's Christmas Eve, it's time."

Into the parlor the family went.
Then the old man read,
"And it came to pass in those days
   that there went out a decree from Caesar Augustus
   that all the world should be taxed . . ."

The candles were lit,
on the tree and on the mantelpiece.

The candles were lit on the windowsills
to light the way of the Christ Child.

And the neighbors came quietly to look,
and to hear the Christmas songs
coming from the house of "the Christmas Family."

As the years went by,
some of the neighbors put candles in their windows too.
Then Christmas trees appeared in their parlors.
They began to sing Christmas songs.
One by one
every household in the village
became a Christmas family.

"O come let us adore Him. O come let us adore Him . . ."